THIS WALKER BOOK
BELONGS TO:

skull

phalanges

sternum

clavicle

mandible

femur

phalanges

metacarpals

scapula

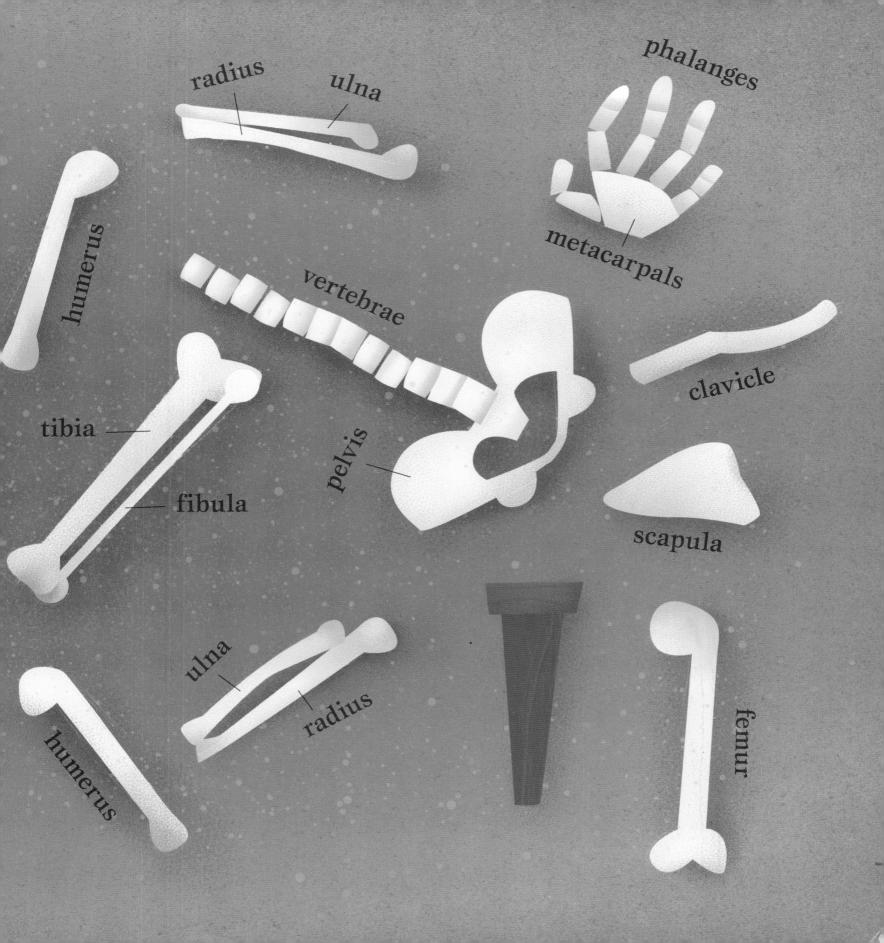

GIVE ME BACK
MY BONES!

KIM NORMAN
illustrated by **BOB KOLAR**

WALKER BOOKS
AND SUBSIDIARIES
LONDON · BOSTON · SYDNEY · AUCKLAND

A stormy night has passed here
and toppled every mast here.
The ocean, flowing fast here,
has scattered all my bones!

Help me find my head bone,
my pillowed-on-the-bed bone,
the pirate's flag-of-dread bone –
I'm scouting out my skull.

Now I need my gnaw bone,
my chicken-chomping saw bone.
I'll starve without my jawbone.
I miss my mandible!

Collar me a collarbone,
the way-down-where-I-swallow bone,
a handy parrot-hauler bone –
I claim my clavicle.

Give me back my breastbone,
the centre-of-my-chest bone,
the hold-my-ribs-the-best bone –
return my sturdy sternum.

Who can spot my shoulder blade,
my shrugging jacket-holder blade,
my shiver-when-I'm-colder blade?
Oh, scapula, come back!

Find my upper arm bone,
the shield-my-face-from-harm bone,
that armpit-of-alarm bone –
I hanker for my humerus.

Don't forget my forearms,
those twisty, wristy chore arms.
I'll jingle-jangle more charms
on radius and ulna.

I'm grasping for some hand bones,
my wave-ahoy-to-land bones
or dig-a-hole-in-sand bones –
I miss my metacarpals.

And still I lack my back bones,
my haul-a-heavy-sack bones,
my strung-up-in-a-stack bones –
return my vertebrae.

Next I need two thighbones,
those top-of-leggy high bones,
my strapping, slapping spry bones.
Has someone seen my femurs?

I'm sunk without my swim pins,
my peg-leg-popping slim pins,
those gangplank-walking shin twins –
called tibia and fibula.

Tickle out my toe bones,
the piggies-in-a-row bones,
my leather-booted low bones –
I miss my fair phalanges.

At last! I've got my lost bones,
no longer skull-and-crossed bones,
my milky ocean-tossed bones...
Avast! I need ...

a ship!

Now, cast a spyglass 'round here
while breakers curl and pound here.
There's treasure to be found here –
I feel it in my bones!

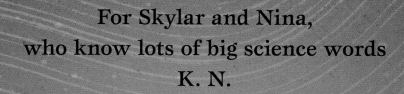

For Skylar and Nina,
who know lots of big science words
K. N.

For Olivia, who helps put lots
of bones back where they belong
B. K.

First published in Great Britain 2019 by Walker Books Ltd
87 Vauxhall Walk, London SE11 5HJ

This edition published 2020

2 4 6 8 10 9 7 5 3 1

Text © 2019 Kim Norman

Illustrations © 2019 Bob Kolar

The right of Kim Norman and Bob Kolar to be identified as the author and illustrator respectively
of this work has been asserted by them in accordance with the Copyright, Designs and Patents Act 1988

This book has been typeset in ITC Esprit Medium

Printed in China

British Library Cataloguing in Publication Data:
a catalogue record for this book is available from the British Library

ISBN 978-1-4063-9296-8

www.walker.co.uk

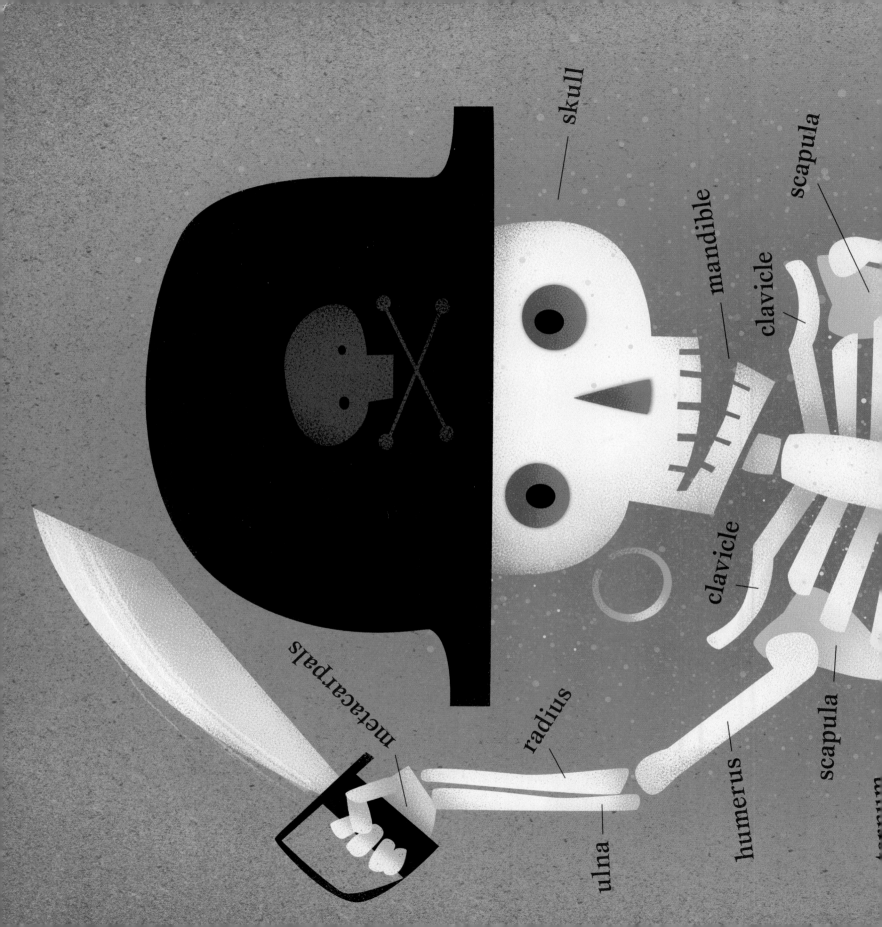

skull

mandible

scapula

clavicle

clavicle

scapula

scapula

humerus

radius

ulna

metacarpals

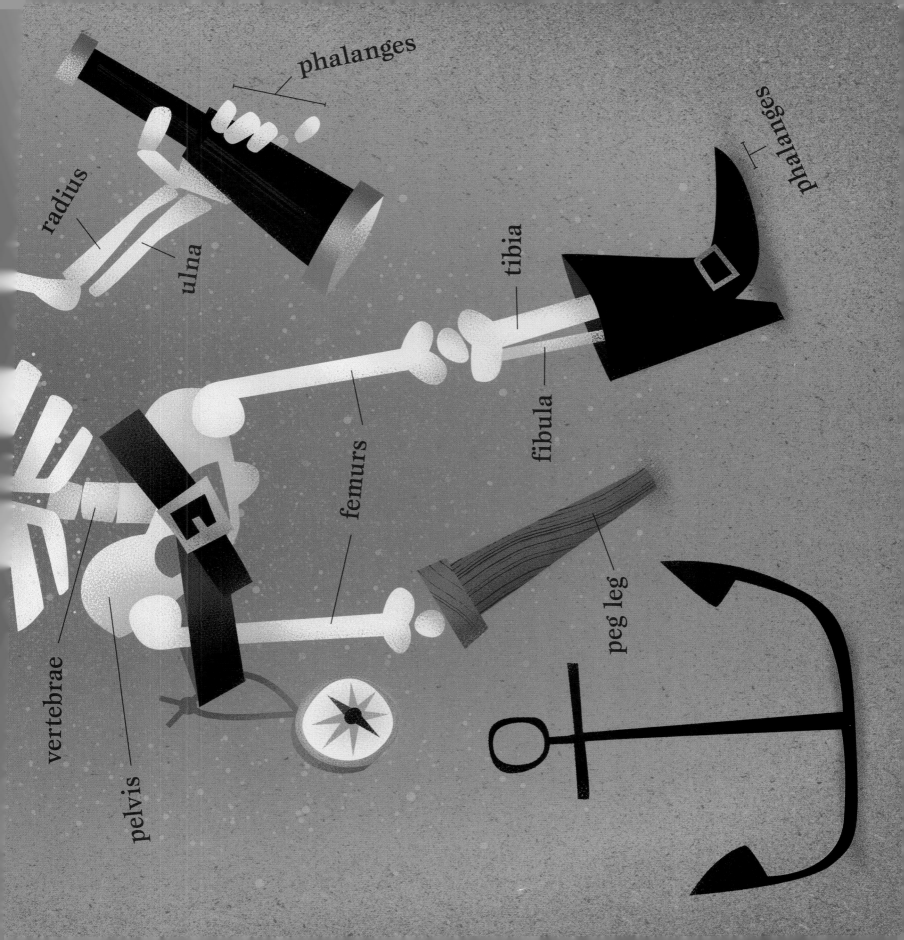

phalanges

phalanges

radius

ulna

tibia

fibula

femurs

peg leg

vertebrae

pelvis

Kim Norman is a poet, writer and graphic artist. She has written many children's books, including *Crocodaddy*, illustrated by David Walker and *Ten on the Sled*, illustrated by Liza Woodruff. Kim loves musical theatre, and once had a paying gig as a singer for a big band. She lives in Virginia, USA, and can be found online at kimnormanbooks.com and on Twitter as @KimNormanAuthor.

Bob Kolar is the author-illustrator of *Big Kicks*. He has also illustrated numerous picture books, including *Slickety Quick: Poems about Sharks,* written by Skila Brown, and *Nothing Like a Puffin,* written by Sue Soltis. Bob Kolar lives in Missouri, USA. Find him online at bobkolarbooks.com.